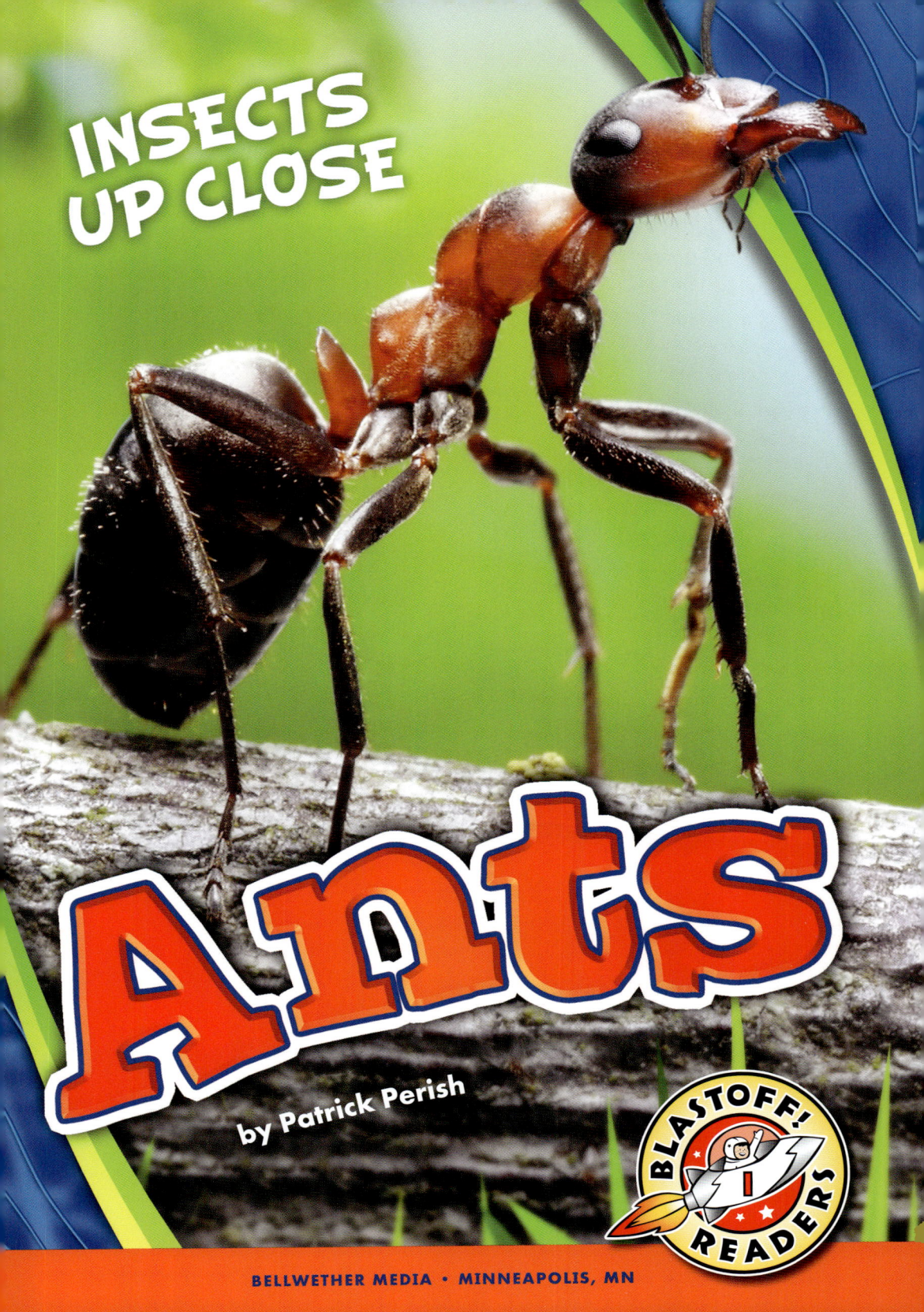

Ants

INSECTS UP CLOSE

by Patrick Perish

BELLWETHER MEDIA • MINNEAPOLIS, MN

Note to Librarians, Teachers, and Parents:

Blastoff! Readers are carefully developed by literacy experts and combine standards-based content with developmentally appropriate text.

Level 1 provides the most support through repetition of high-frequency words, light text, predictable sentence patterns, and strong visual support.

Level 2 offers early readers a bit more challenge through varied simple sentences, increased text load, and less repetition of high-frequency words.

Level 3 advances early-fluent readers toward fluency through increased text and concept load, less reliance on visuals, longer sentences, and more literary language.

Level 4 builds reading stamina by providing more text per page, increased use of punctuation, greater variation in sentence patterns, and increasingly challenging vocabulary.

Level 5 encourages children to move from "learning to read" to "reading to learn" by providing even more text, varied writing styles, and less familiar topics.

Whichever book is right for your reader, Blastoff! Readers are the perfect books to build confidence and encourage a love of reading that will last a lifetime!

This edition first published in 2018 by Bellwether Media, Inc.

No part of this publication may be reproduced in whole or in part without written permission of the publisher. For information regarding permission, write to Bellwether Media, Inc., Attention: Permissions Department, 5357 Penn Avenue South, Minneapolis, MN 55419.

Library of Congress Cataloging-in-Publication Data

Names: Perish, Patrick.
Title: Ants / by Patrick Perish.
Description: Minneapolis, MN : Bellwether Media, Inc., 2018. | Series: Blastoff! Readers. Insects Up Close | Audience: Age 5-8. | Audience: K to grade 3. | Includes bibliographical references and index.
Identifiers: LCCN 2016052737 (print) | LCCN 2016053545 (ebook) | ISBN 9781626176577 (hardcover : alk. paper) | ISBN 9781681033877 (ebook)
Subjects: LCSH: Ants–Juvenile literature.
Classification: LCC QL568.F7 P425 2018 (print) | LCC QL568.F7 (ebook) | DDC 595.79/6–dc23
LC record available at https://lccn.loc.gov/2016052737

Text copyright © 2018 by Bellwether Media, Inc. BLASTOFF! READERS and associated logos are trademarks and/or registered trademarks of Bellwether Media, Inc. SCHOLASTIC, CHILDREN'S PRESS, and associated logos are trademarks and/or registered trademarks of Scholastic Inc.

Editor: Christina Leighton   Designer: Maggie Rosier

Printed in the United States of America, North Mankato, MN.

Table of Contents

What Are Ants?	4
Hard at Work	10
Growing Up	18
Glossary	22
To Learn More	23
Index	24

What Are Ants?

Ants are hard workers. These insects work together for their **colonies**.

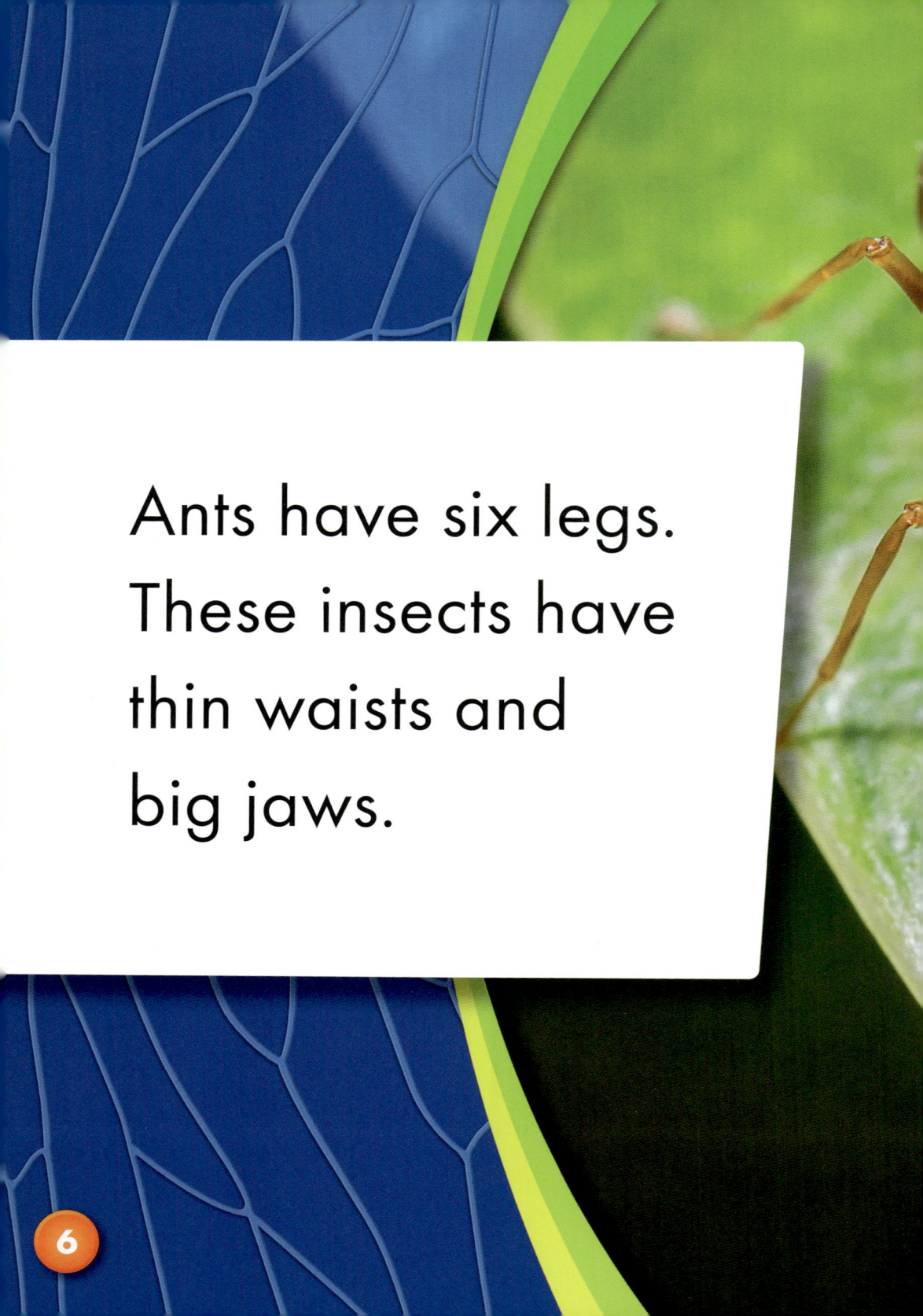

Ants have six legs. These insects have thin waists and big jaws.

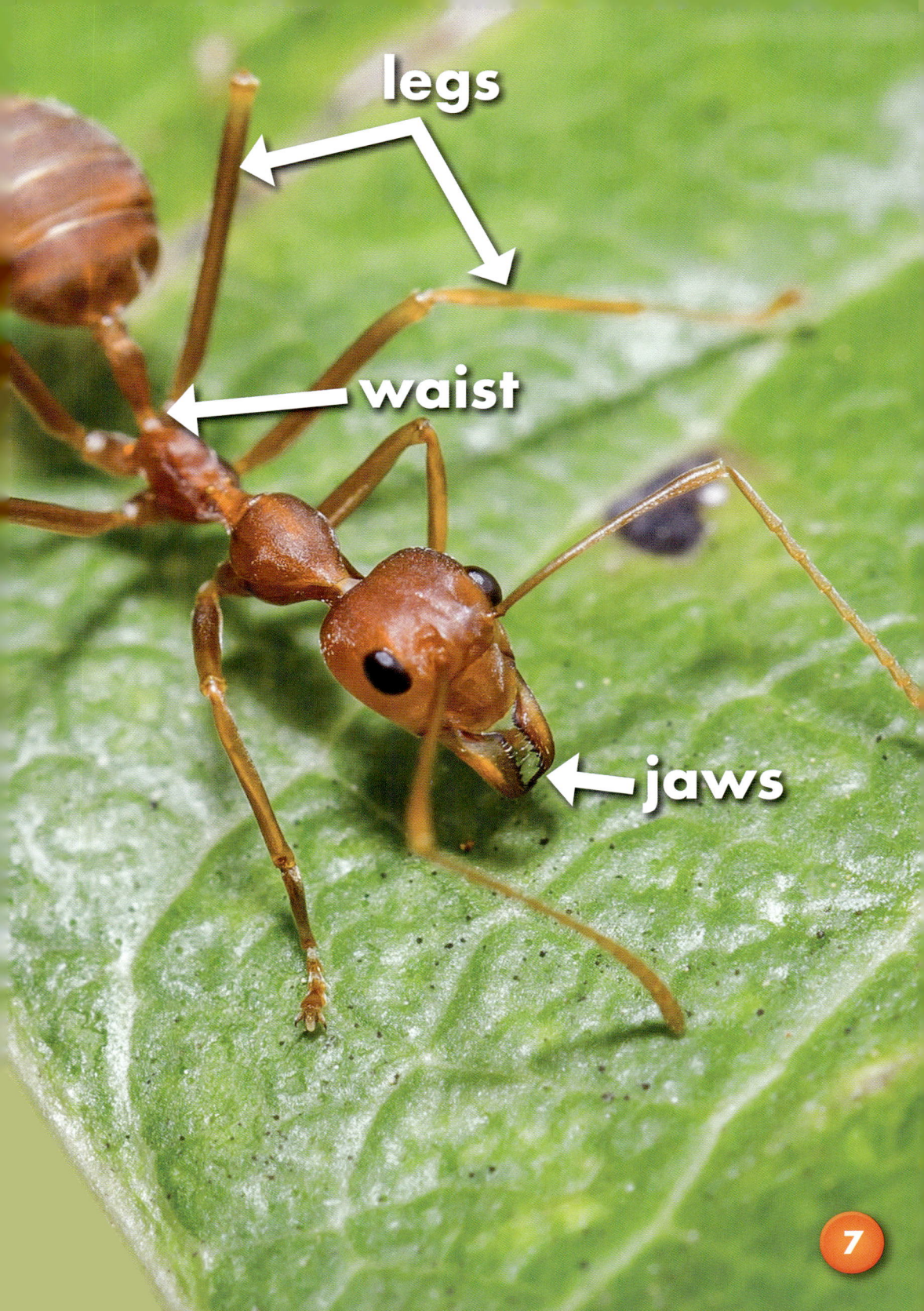

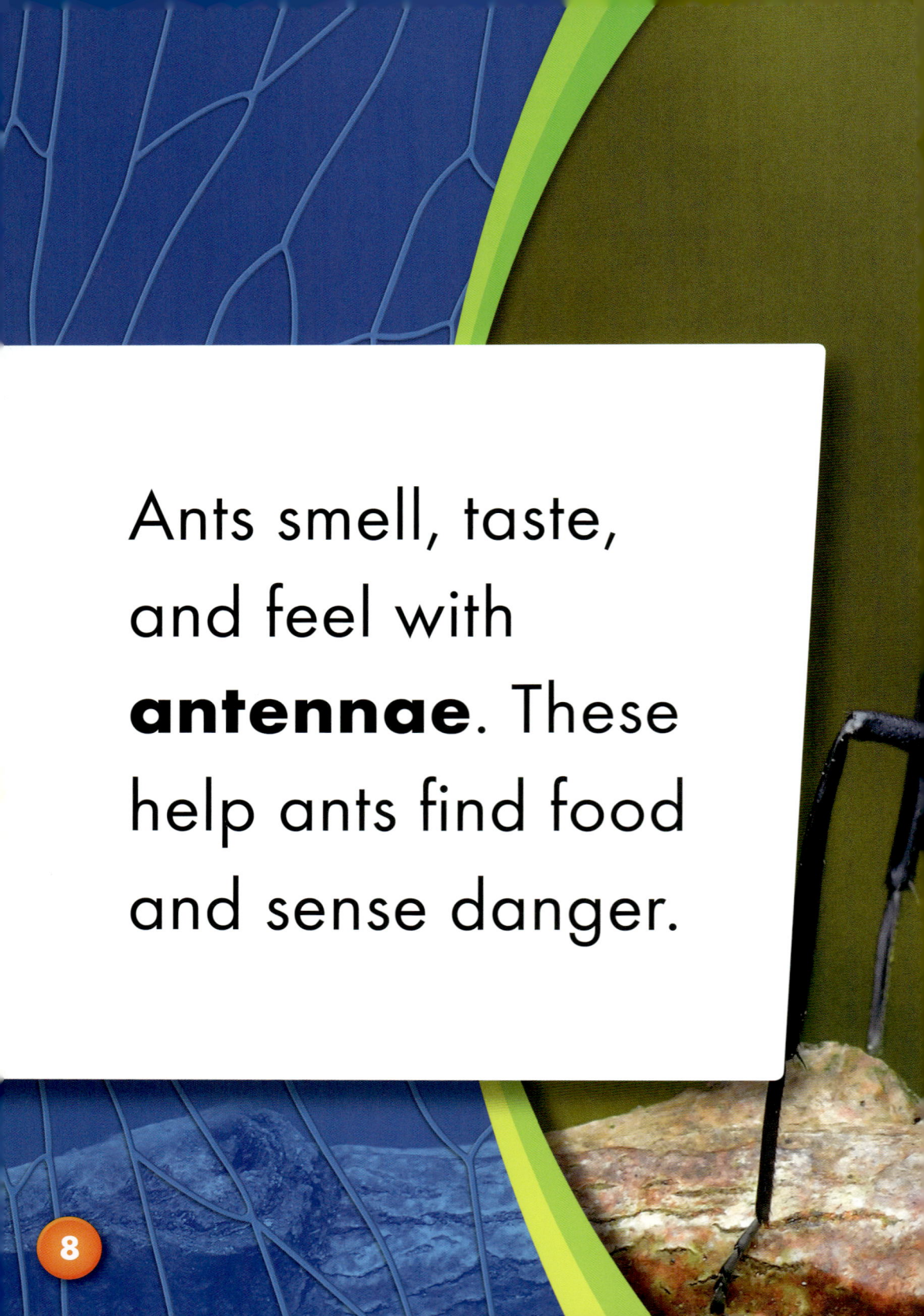

Ants smell, taste, and feel with **antennae**. These help ants find food and sense danger.

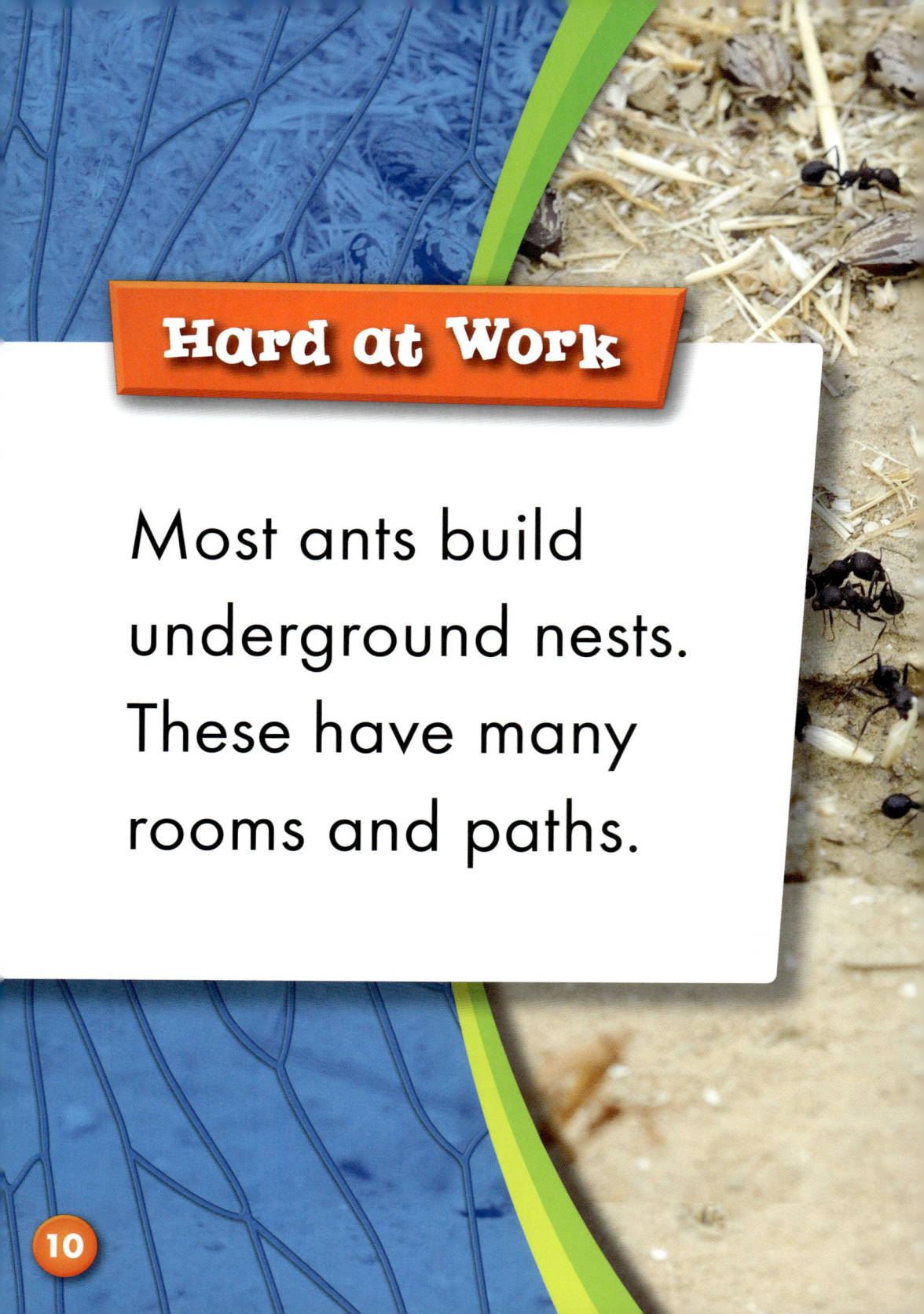

Hard at Work

Most ants build underground nests. These have many rooms and paths.

in the nest

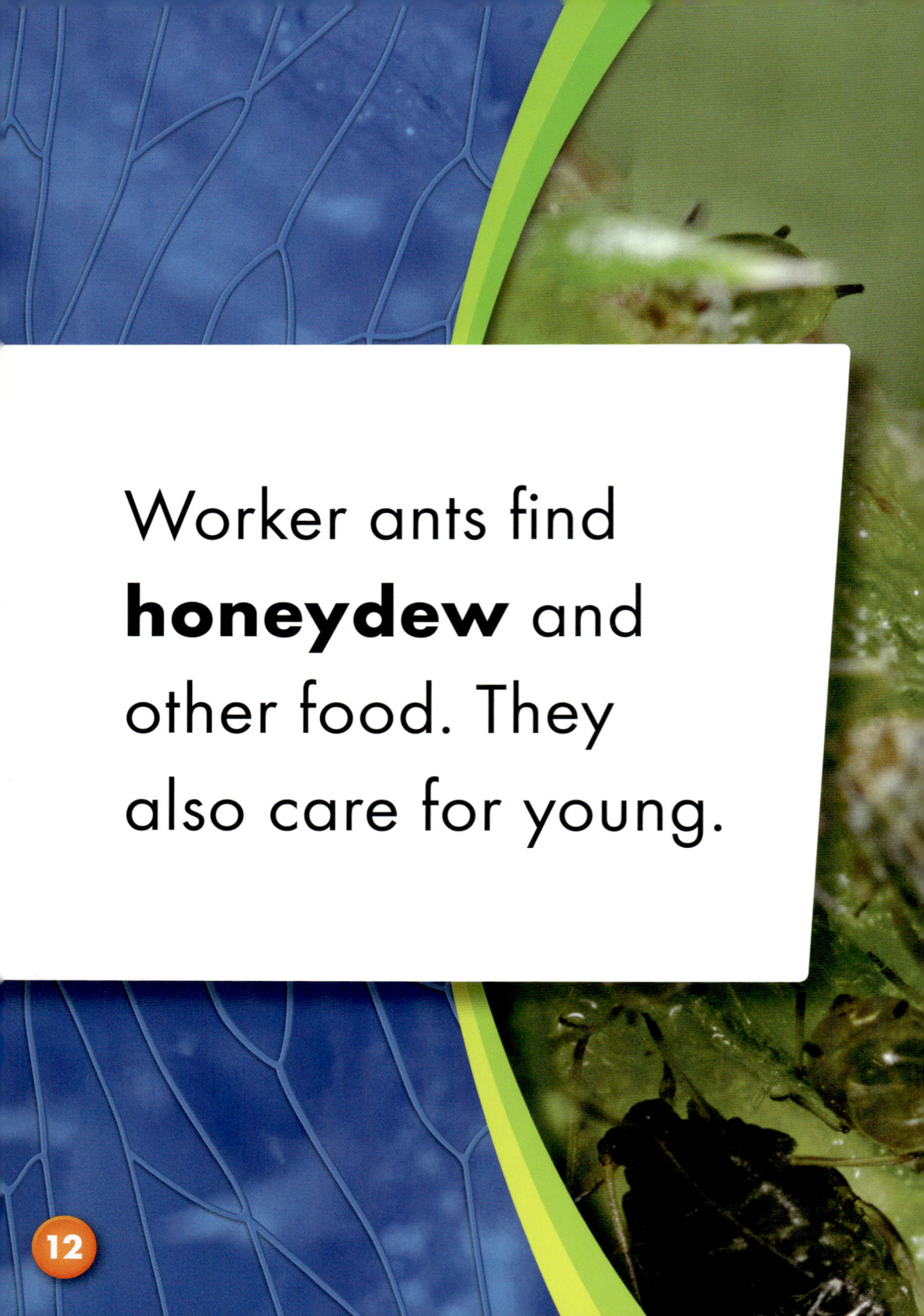

Worker ants find **honeydew** and other food. They also care for young.

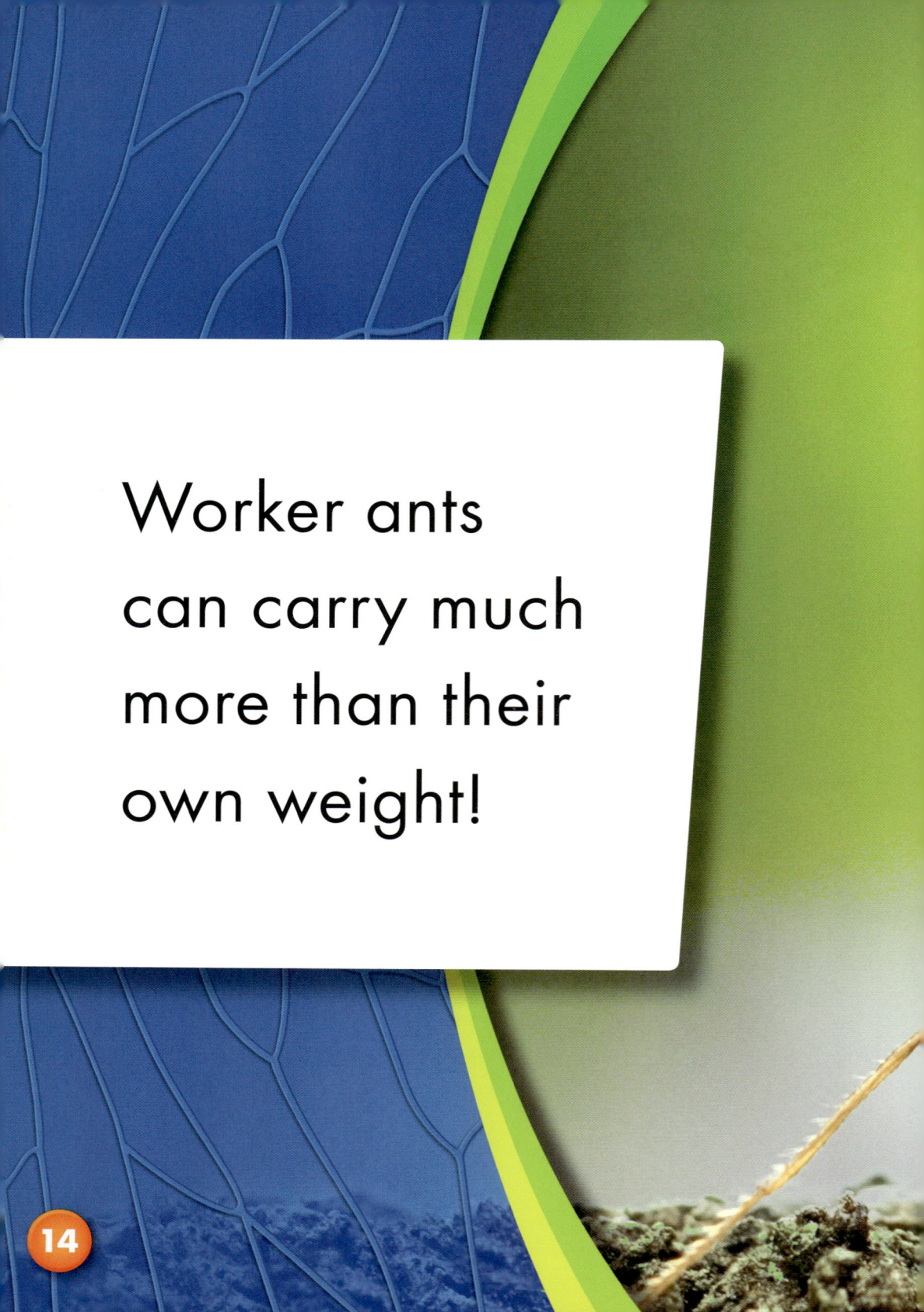

Worker ants can carry much more than their own weight!

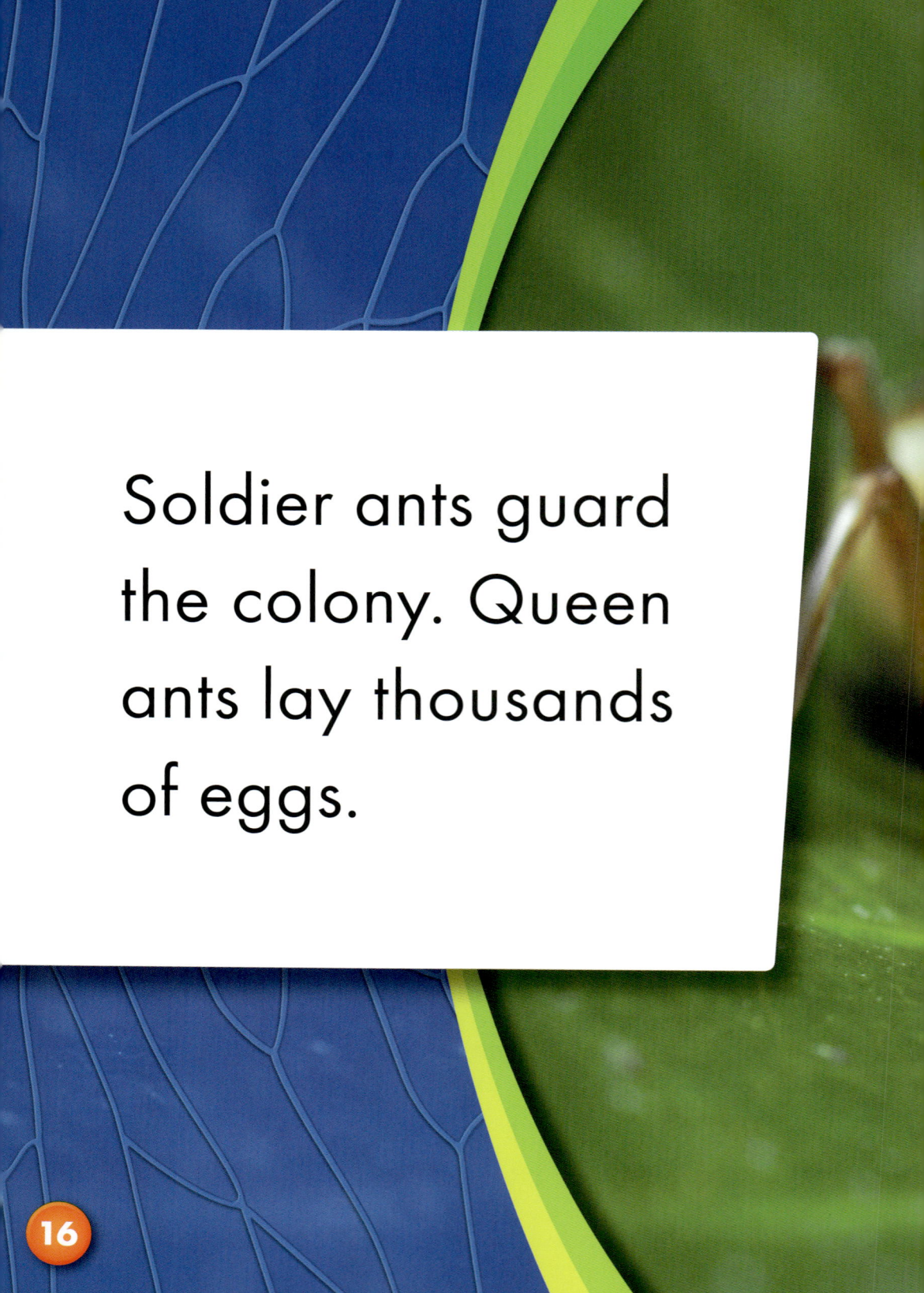

Soldier ants guard the colony. Queen ants lay thousands of eggs.

queen ant

QUEEN ANT LIFE SPAN:
5 to 15 years

↑ eggs

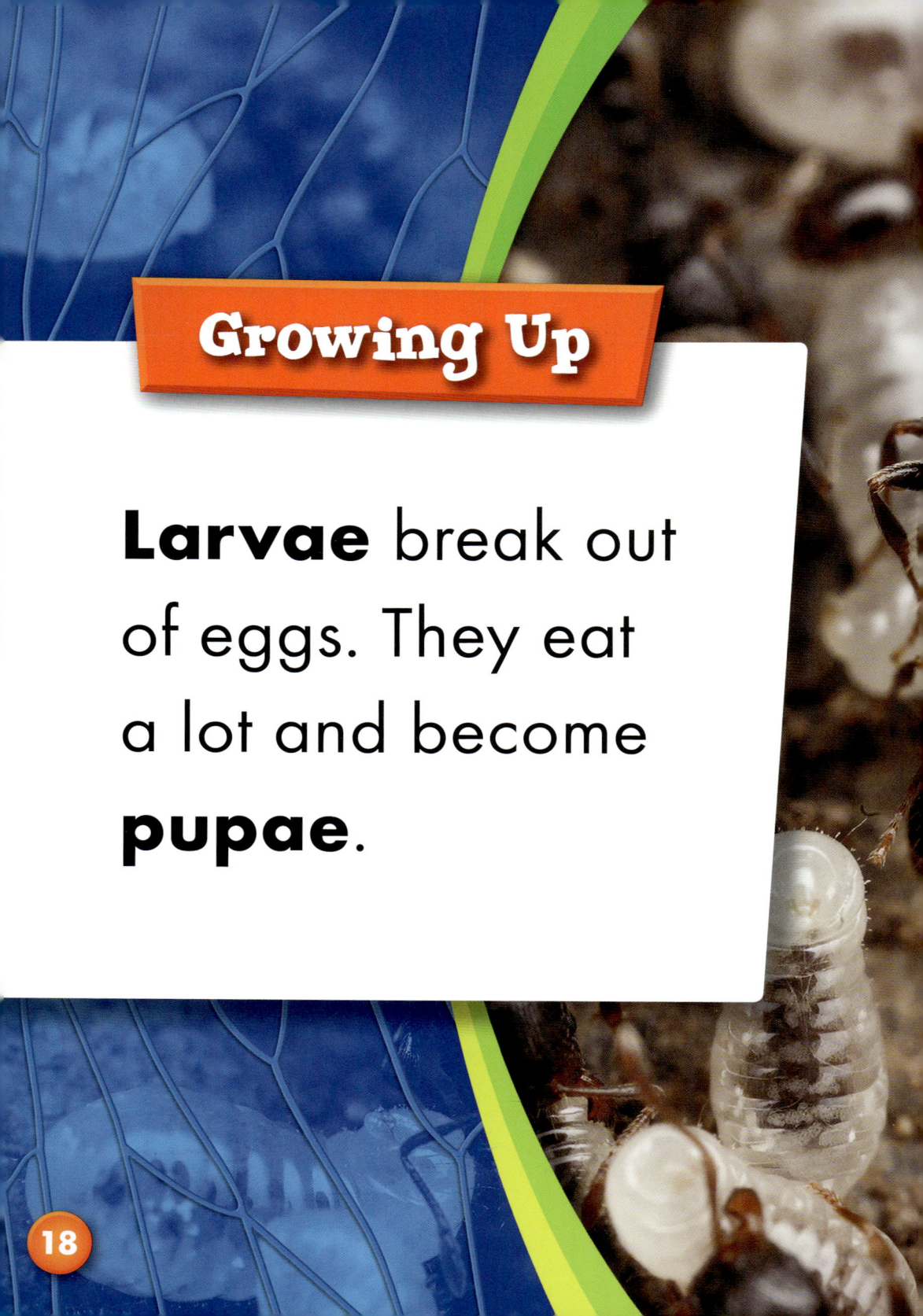

Growing Up

Larvae break out of eggs. They eat a lot and become **pupae**.

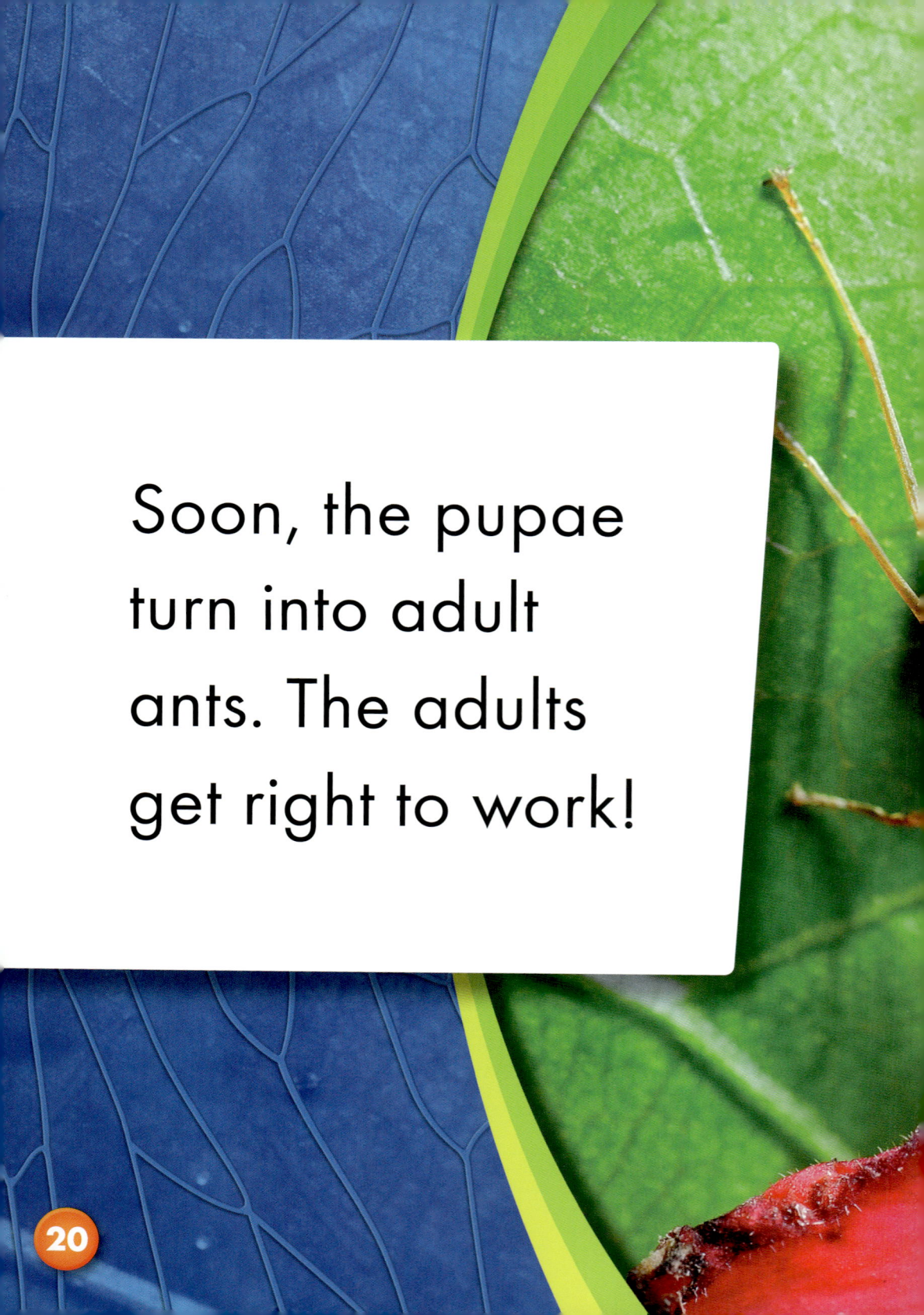

Soon, the pupae turn into adult ants. The adults get right to work!

adult ants

Glossary

antennae

feelers connected to the head that sense information around them

larvae

baby insects that have come from eggs; larvae look like worms.

colonies

large groups of ants that work together to live

pupae

young insects that are about to become adults

honeydew

the sweet liquid some insects make from feeding on plants

To Learn More

AT THE LIBRARY

Amstutz, Lisa. *Ants*. North Mankato, Minn.: Capstone Press, 2017.

Nagle, Frances. *Zombie Ants*. New York, N.Y.: Gareth Stevens Publishing, 2015.

Schuh, Mari. *Ants*. Minneapolis, Minn.: Jump!, 2014.

ON THE WEB

Learning more about ants is as easy as 1, 2, 3.

1. Go to www.factsurfer.com.

2. Enter "ants" into the search box.

3. Click the "Surf" button and you will see a list of related web sites.

With factsurfer.com, finding more information is just a click away.

Index

adult ants, 20, 21
antennae, 8, 9
colonies, 4, 16
danger, 8
eggs, 16, 17, 18
food, 8, 12, 13
honeydew, 12, 13
jaws, 6, 7
larvae, 18, 19
legs, 6, 7
life span, 17
nests, 10, 11
paths, 10
pupae, 18, 19, 20

queen ants, 16, 17
rooms, 10
size, 5
soldier ants, 16
waists, 6, 7
weight, 14
worker ants, 12, 13, 14
young, 12

The images in this book are reproduced through the courtesy of: Andrey Pavlov, front cover; beer worawut, pp. 4-5; Petch A Ratana, pp. 6-7; cylim888, pp. 8-9; AG-PHOTOS, pp. 10-11; Сергей Тряпицын, p. 11; blickwinkel/ Alamy, pp. 12-13; ch123, p. 13; Eric Isselee, pp. 14-15; YoONSpY, pp. 16-17; Pavel Krasensky, pp. 18-19; Henrik Larsson, pp. 19, 22 (top right, bottom right); moomsabuy, pp. 20-21; Jukkapong Piyarom, p. 22 (top left); Meister Photos, p. 22 (center left); Amada44/ Wikipedia, p. 22 (bottom left).